Newcastle

City Council

Newcastle Libraries and Information Service

☏ **0845 002 0336**

Due for return	Due for return	Due for return
1 7 NOV 2009		
— 2 JAN 2010		2 4 SEP 2013
2 8 MAY 2010		— 4 NOV 2014
	— 6 FEB 2010	2 1 NOV 2014
— 3 DEC 2010	1 6 MAR 2010	2 5 NOV 2014
	— 6 APR 2010	
1 5 FEB 2011	3 0 OCT 2010	1 3 FEB 2015
		2 0 JUL 2019
	1 7 MAY 2013	
	— 2 AUG 2013	

Please return this item to any of Newcastle's Libraries by the last date shown above. If not requested by another customer the loan can be renewed, you can do this by phone, post or in person.
Charges may be made for late returns.

For Dawn J.O.

To Lindsey and Rabbit from the girls x L.G.

OXFORD
UNIVERSITY PRESS

Great Clarendon Street, Oxford OX2 6DP

Oxford University Press is a department of the University of Oxford.
It furthers the University's objective of excellence in research, scholarship,
and education by publishing worldwide in

Oxford   New York

Auckland Cape Town Dar es Salaam Hong Kong Karachi
Kuala Lumpur Madrid Melbourne Mexico City Nairobi
New Delhi Shanghai Taipei Toronto

With offices in

Argentina Austria Brazil Chile Czech Republic France Greece
Guatemala Hungary Italy Japan Poland Portugal Singapore
South Korea Switzerland Thailand Turkey Ukraine Vietnam

Oxford is a registered trade mark of Oxford University Press
in the UK and in certain other countries

Text © Jan Ormerod 2005
Illustrations © Lindsey Gardiner 2005

British Library Cataloguing in Publication Data

Data available

ISBN 978-0-19-279140-5 (paperback)

ISBN 978-0-19-271988-1 (paperback with audio CD)

13 15 17 19 20 18 16 14

Printed in China

Doing the Animal BOP

Jan Ormerod and Lindsey Gardiner

IF you like to dance
and you sometimes **sing**,

why don't
you do the
animal thing?

put your heels together, and **waddle** along.

Go Craak Craak Craak – it's the **penguin** song!

High stepping knees
and feathers that
bounce –

flim - flam
flutter
to the **ostrich** flounce.

just like a **snake** you can **slither** along,

Jump and wiggle

to the monkey bop.

Then go hee-haw
hee-haw, too!

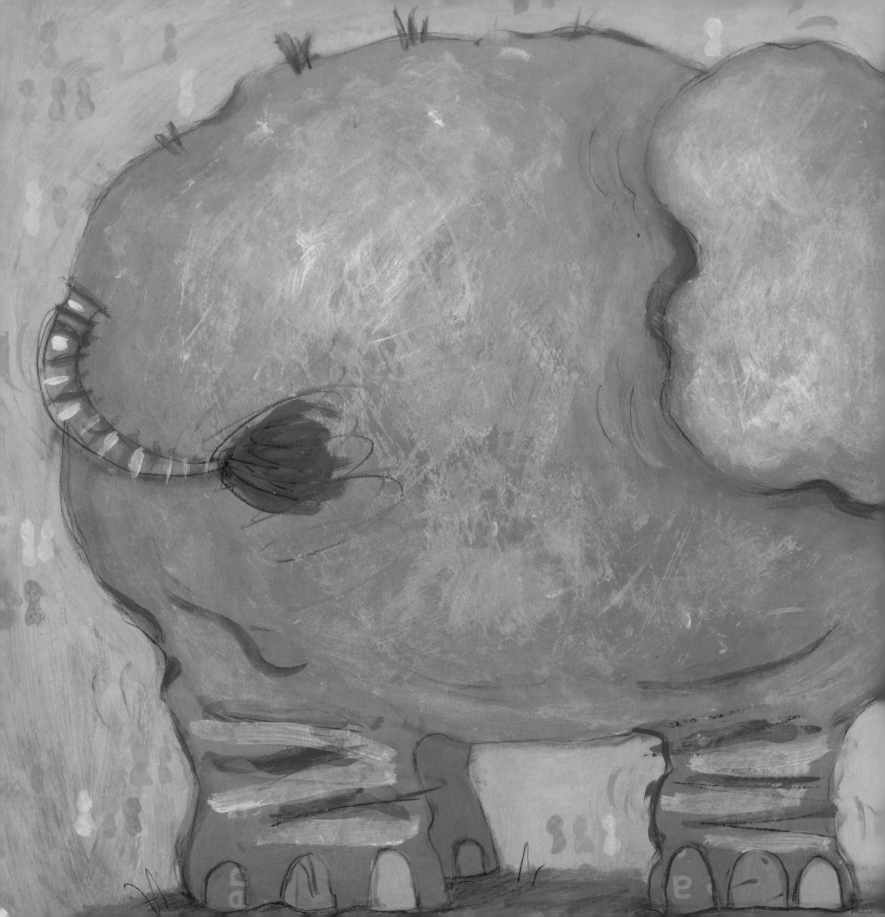

Wave one ARM.

STOMP your feet.

Trudge along to the elephant beat.

Move **one** leg.

Now move **two** . . .

. . . move the way that the **lizards** do.

A chicken can **peck** . . .

... and a chicken can **CLUCK**.

But I think it's more fun
being a **duck** ...

The duck does a **waddle**

on his **FLIP-FLAP** feet,

Roar and rage,

it's a rhino romp!

So let's end up with a great big

mmmmooooooooooooooo